JUST LIKE DADDY

A FRANK ASCH BEAR BOOK

JUST LIKE DADDY

• FRANK ASCH •

ALADDIN

New York London Toronto Sydney New Delhi

ALADDIN

An imprint of Simon & Schuster Children's Publishing Division

1230 Avenue of the Americas, New York, NY 10020

This Aladdin edition April 2015

For information about special discounts for bulk purchases,

please contact Simon & Schuster Special Sales at 1-866-506-1949

or business@simonandschuster.com.

The Simon & Schuster Speakers Bureau can bring authors to your live event.

For more information or to book an event contact the

Simon & Schuster Speakers Bureau at 1-866-248-3049

or visit our website at www.simonspeakers.com.

Designed by Karina Granda

The text of this book was set in Olympian LT Std.

Manufactured in China 0115 SCP

2 4 6 8 10 9 7 5 3 1

Library of Congress Control Number 88-6570

ISBN 978-1-4814-2208-6 (hc)

ISBN 978-1-4814-2207-9 (pbk)

ISBN 978-1-4814-2209-3 (eBook)

To Devin

When I got up this morning,
I yawned a big yawn . . .

Just like Daddy.

I washed my face, got dressed,
and had a big breakfast . . .

Just like
Daddy.

Then I put on my coat
and my boots . . .

Just like Daddy.

And we all went fishing.

On the way I picked a flower
and gave it to my mother . . .

Just like Daddy.

When we got to the lake, I put a
big worm on my hook . . .

Just like Daddy.

All day we fished and fished,

and I caught a big fish . . .

Just like Mommy!